Bleep peeks into an open door.

Bloop pushes a silver thing.

The Crater Heads have their first new sound. And what a sound it is!

Then they saw some things walking fast into a big place.

Look at them. What do you think they are doing?

Why are they rushing like that? They must be going to do something fun!

Well, we will not learn much standing here like craters on a moon. Come on!

The Crater Heads have a little too much fun trying to get past the door.

Make them stop!

I am late!

I have to go to a meeting!

When they get inside, they hear sounds everywhere!

More sweet sounds!

RING

RING

RING RING RING

TAP TAP TAP

BEEP BEEP BEEP

MY BROTHER IS AN ALIEN

One day, Dirk was making funny faces in the mirror at his baby brother.

Dirk sees something odd.

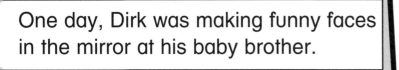

I saw something sticking out of his head!

What are you saying? You can see that your brother is fine.